BIONICLE®

City of the Lost

BIONICLE®

FIND THE POWER,

LIVE THE LEGEND

The legend comes alive in these exciting BIONICLE® books:

BIONICLE Chronicles
#1 Tale of the Toa
#2 Beware the Bohrok
#3 Makuta's Revenge
#4 Tales of the Masks

BIONICLE: Mask of Light
The Official Guide to BIONICLE
BIONICLE Collector's Sticker Book
BIONICLE: Metru Nui: City of Legends
BIONICLE: Rahi Beasts
BIONICLE: Dark Hunters

BIONICLE Adventures
#1 Mystery of Metru Nui
#2 Trial by Fire
#3 The Darkness Below
#4 Legends of Metru Nui
#5 Voyage of Fear

#6 Maze of Shadows
#7 Web of the Visorak
#8 Challenge of the Hordika
#9 Web of Shadows
#10 Time Trap

BIONICLE Legends
#1 Island of Doom
#2 Dark Destiny
#3 Power Play

#4 Legacy of Evil
#5 Inferno
#6 City of the Lost

BIONICLE®

City of the Lost

by Greg Farshtey

SCHOLASTIC INC.
New York Toronto London Auckland Sydney
Mexico City New Delhi Hong Kong Buenos Aires

For my sister Debbie, who always found me whenever I was lost.

ISBN-13: 978-0-439-89033-5
ISBN-10: 0-439-89033-0

12 11 10 9 8 7 6 5 4 3   7 8 9 10 11/0

Printed in the U.S.A.
First printing, February 2007

 # PROLOGUE

80,000 Years Ago

Pridak stood on the tower of his island fortress, looking down at his assembled army. His troops came from an endless number of places. Some were Matoran criminals, others violent brutes looking for the chance to fight, and by far the majority were simply beings who were no longer welcome in their homelands. They were thieves, murderers, traitors, and liars, and easily the most beautiful sight he had ever seen.

He shifted his gaze to the west. There, Takadox's and Mantax's armies had set up camp. To the east, the legions of Kalmah and Ehlek were preparing for battle. Carapar's army was the last to arrive and they had immediately begun skirmishing with some of the others. No effort had been made to stop them. It was best they keep their weapons and their battle instincts sharp for what was to come.

Pridak took a deep breath. The air smelled sweet. He wanted to savor these last few moments of his old life. Soon, he would no longer be just the ruler of a small realm, one almost beneath the notice of the Great Spirit Mata Nui. Before this day was through, he would be the undisputed king of one-sixth of the known universe.

If it were possible for a biomechanical being to be a perfect physical specimen, Pridak was it. Even if his armor and weapons had been taken away, he would still have radiated power. It was hard for him to comprehend how some beings, even entire intelligent species, could live out their lives with monstrous appearances. He imagined they must just be dead inside and so didn't notice the horror they inspired.

A strong wind set the island's trees to swaying. The scent of campfires, unwashed Matoran, and Rahi mounts combined into a musty, foul aroma. The smell triggered memories of past conquests. They had been hard-fought battles, and well worth winning, but they could not compare with what he and his allies were about to undertake.

One of his battle leaders approached. "Sir, all is ready. We await your order to strike."

Pridak nodded, his keen eyes trained on his legions below. "Indeed. Three members of a Matoran rear guard unit have propped their weapons against rocks and are having a conversation among themselves. Why?"

The battle leader turned to look. Then, flustered, he answered, "I . . . have no explanation, sir. They will be disciplined at once."

A tight smile appeared on Pridak's face. "Three ignore their orders while their fifty companions stand at attention and do nothing about it. Not at all satisfactory."

He turned to the battle leader. "Pass the word among my legions. That unit is to be attacked and completely destroyed, immediately . . . along with you."

"What? Sir, I . . . I . . ."

Pridak's hand flashed out and grabbed the

battle leader by the throat. He took two quick strides and thrust the unfortunate being over the edge of the tower. His captive's legs dangled in space.

"Am I speaking some unknown Matoran dialect?" Pridak whispered. "Do you require a translator? I want you to go down there and order your own destruction. I want you to do it now."

Pridak leaned in close, his fetid breath washing over his frightened subordinate. "Be assured my legions will be far swifter and more merciful in carrying out their task than I would be."

With that, Pridak idly tossed the battle leader back onto the stone floor of the tower. The panicked being scrambled to his feet and raced down the stairs to carry out his orders. When he reached the bottom, he would command the legions to immediately wipe out the offending unit and then himself. He would do this because he knew Pridak was right. Death at their hands would be far preferable to the same fate in the clutches of his ruler.

* * *

The other five Barraki were waiting in the fortress's central chamber, studying maps carved into stone tablets. They had been given their name centuries ago by the subjects of their realms. It was an old Matoran word, rarely ever heard, which roughly translated to "warlord." Each was powerful, well armored, and veteran of many a raid. Those who saw them said they made Toa look like some kind of Rahi that crawled out from under a rock. They saw themselves as a higher level of being, preordained to rule by virtue of their superior strength and intellect.

The charts they looked over were rough, but they were good enough for the Barraki's purposes. One set of tablets showed key points on the central continent. The other covered the sea approaches to the city of Metru Nui.

"Guarded here, here, here," said Ehlek. His nerves were obvious. Although he reigned on land, Ehlek's species was native to a watery realm. He was able to function on the surface only through a complicated apparatus that enabled him to breathe air. That made him vulnerable and he knew it.

"We'll surround and crush them," Kalmah said, impatient to get started.

Takadox shook his head. "No. We let them see an advance scouting party, then lure them into a trap."

Carapar and Mantax said nothing, one because he had nothing useful to add and the other because he did not want his allies to know his strategies.

"Toa," said Kalmah, as dismissively as if he were discussing the weather. "They are a moment's annoyance, at best."

"Easy for you to say," Takadox shot back. "I was there when they 'annoyed' a Kanohi Dragon into submission. For what is at stake, they will fight, and to the death."

Pridak's voice was a sharpened sword wrapped in soft reeds. "Yes. Remember what is at stake, all of you. This is not some petty raid on another realm. These are the sites of true power.

When they fall, Mata Nui himself falls . . . and the universe will answer to us."

Further conversation was interrupted by the sounds of screaming and yelling from outside the fortress, punctuated by the harsh noises of weapon striking weapon. Carapar rushed to the window. He took a quick glance at the scene below and said, "I think the answer came early."

Pridak and the others joined him to view a shocking scene. A massive army had suddenly appeared from the north and slammed into the legions. The attackers were Toa, Exo-Toa machines, Rahkshi, and Rahi beasts, an invading force tens of thousands strong. Unprepared to mount a defense, the Barraki's legions were falling like stone walls before a Kikanalo stampede. But that wasn't what filled the Barraki with a sense of dread. No, that came from the sight of the banner the invaders carried overhead.

It was the symbol of the Brotherhood of Makuta.

There was no time to wonder how the Brotherhood had learned of their plans, or why those defenders of Mata Nui and the Matoran had chosen to leave their bases and attack. The Barraki rushed out to take command of their legions and try to organize some kind of defense. Each knew that those captured by the Brotherhood, especially in an act of open rebellion against the Great Spirit, could expect no mercy. Death in battle was by far the better alternative.

The battle was over by nightfall. The Barraki's troops were tough, good fighters, but they weren't as well disciplined as the Brotherhood's army. Taken by surprise and outmaneuvered, large numbers of them deserted or surrendered. But the leader of the victorious force did not care about them. He wanted their leaders.

The Barraki fought to the last but were finally overpowered. They were brought in chains to the front of their ranks. Then, for the first time, they saw their conqueror. It was the Makuta who guarded Metru Nui and its surrounding area. His power and genius were known throughout the universe. A lesser being would never have been placed in charge of so vital a region.

Makuta looked at the Barraki with cold, crimson eyes, as if they were insects he was looking forward to crushing. They, in turn, looked right back at him, even Ehlek. After all, they were not some petty criminals who quaked at the sight of a Toa or even a Brotherhood member. They were rulers. They were warriors. And they were Barraki.

"Your rebellion is over," Makuta said. "Your misguided attempt to overthrow the Great Spirit is now history . . . as are you."

Makuta walked down the line of prisoners and stopped at Pridak. "These others I am not familiar with, but you . . . you I know. Why?"

"I served the Brotherhood in days long past," Pridak answered, not at all intimidated by Makuta's presence. "In fact, it was the Brotherhood who gave me my first command. Oh, it was a small territory, barely worth controlling. But I have since moved on to bigger things."

"So I see," Makuta murmured under his breath.

"What will happen to us now?" asked Takadox. "You know, our armies could be of use to you, great Makuta. Combined with the might of yours, Mata Nui could not hope to —"

Makuta took two steps forward and struck Takadox, hard, with an armored hand. The Barraki went sprawling in the dirt. "Your every word condemns you," said Makuta, rage contorting his features. "There is only one possible fate for such traitors."

The automated Exo-Toa armored suits took aim with their weapons. Those few Toa who were nearby raised their voices in protest. Makuta ignored them. But before he could give the order to fire, a new element entered the picture.

A lone figure was approaching, tall, powerful, with a face so hideous it would give nightmares to a Visorak. Even Makuta seemed taken aback by the newcomer.

"I am Botar," the figure said. "The Pit calls, and I have come."

"What?" asked Makuta. "Who summoned you? What business do you have here?"

"The business of punishment," Botar replied, "although to call it an art would not be far wrong."

"You have no rights here," Makuta snarled. "Begone."

Botar smiled, a monstrous grin. "Where there are wrongs, Makuta . . . I have rights. Stand aside."

"I will not! These are my prisoners."

Botar continued to smile, but his voice grew dark and filled with menace. "Stand aside or share their fate."

The nightmarish figure gestured toward the Barraki. A ring of energy appeared around them, tendrils of power connecting it to Botar. Before Makuta could act, all seven — the six Barraki and Botar — had faded away. All that was left behind was the echo of the Barraki's screams.

In the months to come, the Barraki's legions and their empires were broken up. Some of their troops were sent back to their home islands for imprisonment, others were taken by the Brotherhood as slave laborers. The Barraki's fortresses were torn down and the stones ground to powder. The names of the warlords were expunged from every chronicle, with the exception of the Brotherhood's roll of victory.

The fate of the six traitors remained a mystery, even to Makuta. Sometimes, in the dark of night, he would remember the look in Pridak's cold, dead eyes, and some part of him would hope the Barraki were dead. Along with that wish would come other thoughts, ones that would occupy his mind more and more as time passed.

The Barraki believed Mata Nui could be overthrown and replaced. Of course, it could never be done by the likes of them, Makuta said to himself. *But who is to say it could never be done at all?*

And somewhere in the endless darkness of the Pit, the Barraki waited, and brooded, and longed for the day they would take revenge. . . .

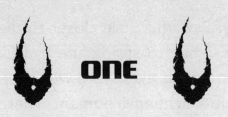

ONE

Reysa stood impatiently at the edge of the fields of air, waiting for his herd of hydruka to finish their work. The Onu-Matoran knew that the creatures could not be rushed. Although tame, they were still highly temperamental. If they chose to be stubborn and not harvest the airweed, he would have a lot of explaining to do when he got back to the city.

Still, he wished they would hurry up. Looking like a cross between a crab and a scorpion, they moved slowly through the field, gathering the weeds one at a time. It wasn't particularly difficult work — a Matoran could do it, easily — but only the hydruka could tell which weeds contained precious air and which did not. For Reysa and the other Matoran who lived in the underwater city of Mahri Nui, air was the most valuable commodity imaginable.

Reysa swam a little closer to the field, trying his best not to spook the hydruka. Like all Onu-Matoran, his eyes were well suited to operating in a low-light environment. There were few places darker than the outskirts of Mahri Nui. The only one Reysa could name was the watery region just below the city. The darkness there might as well have been a reflection of the hearts of its inhabitants.

That thought made him swim closer to the hydruka and wave his arms to urge them on. He had foolishly lost track of how long they had been at work. If the safe hour was almost over — or worse, had already passed — every moment he spent this far from the city put his life at risk.

There might be something down below right now, watching me, he thought. *I know how they watch, with those cold, milky eyes. I know what's happened to those who didn't make it back before safe hour ended . . . or I can guess.*

He looked around but could see nothing out of the ordinary. Just the vast underwater world and a few schools of fish swimming idly by . . . not even any marine predators around. That was good. It meant there might still be time left in the hour. If the hydruka would just hurry up . . .

Come on! he shouted in his mind. *What's taking so long? If they weren't simply Rahi, I would think they take some pleasure out of making me worry like this.*

He heard a sharp noise from below and to his left. It stood out from the constant cacophony of sounds that filled the undersea realm, for it sounded like metal scraping against rock. Reysa wondered if it might be some piece of equipment that had drifted away from the city and become lodged in the rocks below. Maybe it would be something worth recovering.

Mahri Nui and the fields of air rested on a large, mountainous slab of rock that looked like an upside-down triangle. The base of the triangle was at the top and was where the city was located. The point of the triangle was at the bottom, wedged between some massive, curved bars of rock. If it weren't, or if it ever became dislodged, Mahri Nui's chunk of solid ground would tumble end over end to the very bottom of the ocean, taking all of the Matoran with it.

Reysa began to swim toward the edge of the undersea island. When he was almost there, he stopped. *What am I doing?* he said to himself. *I've heard enough tales of "quick peeks" over the side that led to disaster. Whatever is scraping against the rocks can just stay there, as far as I'm concerned. I just want to get these hydruka and their harvest back to the city.*

He turned away from the precipice, normally a good thing. After all, if beyond the edge lies danger, reversing your course and moving away from it would keep one safe. Except, of course, that it makes it impossible to see what might be coming after you from behind.

That was why Reysa was so surprised to feel a tentacle wrapping around his chest. It began to pull him back toward the edge as if he were no more than an errant piece of airweed. He swam, he kicked, he struggled, but all he accomplished was to panic the hydruka.

Reysa was over the edge now, with nothing but black water below him. He beat on the tentacle with his fists, then kicked backward. His foot struck something solid — it had to be the body of the creature!

He looked over his shoulder, hoping to at least have the satisfaction of knowing what was dragging him off to his doom. He looked, and he saw, and then he discovered a basic fact of life (and death): The problem with being underwater is that you can't scream.

Defilak walked silently into the Matoran Council chamber. Located deep inside the Mahri Nui fortress, it was the largest single room in the entire settlement. The huge, domed ceiling featured crystal skylights lined with lightstones whose gleam reflected off the water all around. The walls of the chamber were lined with "Mata Nui's gifts" — tools and artifacts that drifted down through the ocean to Mahri Nui every month, from no one knew where. Those items that could be put to use were given to the Matoran most in need, and the rest were brought here to be mounted.

But what truly gave the chamber its air of solemnity and importance was its purpose. Here every Matoran citizen would gather once a month to discuss any issues that threatened the safety of the city. Plans were made, decisions arrived at, and hopefully everyone left knowing exactly what the city needed them to do. This was essential to survival in a hostile environment. Leadership of the Council was rotated among the citizens, and this month Defilak was in charge.

He took his place on the raised platform and looked out over the assembled Matoran. His friend Gar smiled and nodded encourage-ment. Defilak was many things — an inventor, a scholar — but a public speaker he was not, and he dreaded the experience.

"Um . . . fellow Matoran . . . um," he began. "This talk-meeting will, uh, come to order, please."

The Matoran crowd continued to talk

among themselves, few even noticing that Defilak was standing there.

Defilak tried again. "Hello? Could you all stop the chatter-noise, please, so we can get started?"

The murmur died down a little bit, but not by much. Most of the citizens were still deep in their own private conversations with their neighbors.

Okay, I tried it the nice way twice, Defilak said to himself. *Now I do it my way.*

He slammed his sword down hard on the table, and yelled, "Shut up!"

The crowd quieted instantly and turned to face him, looking shocked. Matoran Council meetings didn't usually start this way, although they occasionally ended with a lot of yelling and now and then a fight.

"That's better," said Defilak. "Does anyone have any word-news to bring before the Council?"

One Po-Matoran rose. "I do. Two of my

friends disappeared today. One was taken from the fields of air, and one tried to reach the world above and never came back . . . that makes five who have vanished in the last two weeks. What are we doing about it?"

Defilak paused before answering. Working in the fields of air was always treacherous because it exposed Matoran to whatever lurked outside the city. But he had thought the residents had enough sense by now not to try to head for the surface. Even if they didn't run out of air, the change in pressure would kill them.

Finally, he said, "Gar? What's the status of our defenses?"

"The razorcrabs are dispersed all along the borders of the city," Gar replied. "The thornplants are intact. Sea creatures have made probing attacks at a few of the outlying shelters, but we drove them back. No organized assaults on the city in two months now."

"Then why can't we travel outside the city in safety?" one Matoran in the crowd demanded.

"That's right!" said another. "We know something is out there, hunting us, killing us, trying to seize and destroy our city. And all we've done is hide in our shelters and hope they go away! Why don't we fight?"

A Ta-Matoran rose to speak. "I wish we could fight and bring down our enemies. But how do we find them? They might be anywhere in the black sea below us, a region they know and we don't. There might be a dozen of them or a hundred. What have any of us ever seen? A tentacle? A claw? Sea life that might be acting like an organized army, or might not? I will be the first to volunteer to fight for Mahri Nui, but first, show me what to fight!"

Defilak gazed up through the skylight windows. The slight blurring of the lightstones' glow showed where a thin bubble of air surrounded the building. That bubble, so vital and so fragile, symbolized Matoran life in Mahri Nui. They were hanging on here, just barely, never knowing when the next attack might come or if the fields of air might suddenly turn barren. Just as they did in the safe hour, every Matoran spent his life waiting for the moment that Mahri Nui's time would run out.

It had not always been this way, he was certain. Just about all of the Matoran had some fragmentary memories of a life on the surface. Some of the memories were pleasant ones, others disturbing and frightening. Regardless, on the rare occasion someone was able to string together a coherent recollection, it was treated as a major event.

But his job was to focus on the here and now. Mahri Nui was under the sea and beset by enemies, whose identity and purpose were still unknown even after centuries of warfare. The Matoran could remain "secure" inside their air bubble protected shelters and wait for the enemy's next move. Or they could go out and find the one weapon that might help them: knowledge.

Defilak rapped his sword three times on the table, indicating it was time for a vote. "I propose a scout-expedition into the black water, to be led by me," he said. "We will quick-learn whatever we can about what's down there and then return. I call for a vote."

Those who supported the measure raised their right hands, those who opposed raised their left. Defilak's proposal passed, though by a closer vote than he had expected. It seemed many of the citizens preferred staying quiet and not antagonizing whatever lurked beyond the city.

"Done," said Defilak. "I need volunteers. We will leave as quick-soon as possible."

"Wait a minute," said Gar. "How do we get down there?"

Defilak smiled. "Oh, I think I can help with that."

Kyrehx, a Ga-Matoran sentry, stood on guard on the borders of the city. A single step would take her outside of the air bubble and into the ocean, where she would be prey to ocean currents and sea predators. Although a personal air bubble would allow her to breathe for a short time, it was doubtful she would survive outside for long.

Not for the first time, she marveled at the way the air bubbles worked. Permeable enough to allow objects to pass through, they somehow managed to keep the sea out. Had Mahri Nui not crashed so near the fields of air, unleashing scores of small bubbles, no Matoran would ever have survived long enough to create bubbles around the buildings and pump the water out.

Unfortunately, the bubbles had a finite existence. Unless reinforced, they would eventually begin to shrink and then disappear completely, allowing the sea to flood entire buildings. It was only the air harvested from the fields by the hydruka and fed into the bubbles that allowed Mahri Nui to remain intact and habitable.

Something caught Kyrehx's eye. An object was floating down toward the city. Gifts from the Great Spirit Mata Nui were not due for some days, so she assumed it was just a piece of debris. That assumption was weakened when she noticed the glow around the artifact. It vanished completely when she heard something call to her in her mind.

Heedless of the danger, she propelled

herself off the rocky surface and through the air bubble. The object was just seconds away from drifting down past the edge of the undersea island and disappearing into the black waters below. She swam faster than she ever had before and grabbed it, then turned and raced for the safety of the bubble.

It was only when she was back at her post that she took the time to examine her find. The light that surrounded it was unearthly, somehow both frightening and calming at the same time. Energy surged from it, so that she felt as if she was struggling to hold on to an electric eel.

Kyrehx's eyes widened. She was holding a Kanohi mask, one she had never seen before. It was no ordinary mask, she could tell that already, and she knew that she must bring it to the Council at once.

What she could not know, as she rushed for the Council chamber, was that she was carrying the legendary Kanohi Mask of Life. Nor could she comprehend that its arrival would herald the beginning of the end for Mahri Nui.

* * *

The dull, white eyes of a Rahi squid narrowed at the sight of the Ga-Matoran sentry passing through the bubble into the ocean. It was hungry for life energy and here was a Matoran offering herself up as a meal. It started to propel itself through the water, ready to strike.

Then the squid stopped. The Matoran had grabbed something drifting in the water. Even with its limited intelligence, and at a great distance, the creature could sense power. This was something that would need to be reported to its master.

It darted down into the black water, heading for the deepest parts of the Pit.

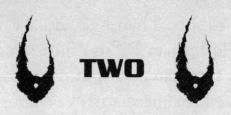

TWO

"You have to be joking," said Gar, shaking his head.

"I hope not, cause you're not happy-laughing," Defilak replied. "My jokes are usually better than that."

"When did you get permission to build this thing?"

"Remember, about a year ago, that Po-Matoran was running the Council — I don't easy-remember his name. You know, the one who was always cracking rocks between his fingers? Anyway, everyone knows Po-Matoran ever-hate the water and anything to do with it, but they're nuts about geology. Give them a boulder to chop-carve and they're happy as hydruka on an air spree."

"Is there a point buried here somewhere?" asked Gar.

"Well, I told him I could build something that would let him go search for rocks to his heartlight's content, without ever having to get his feet wet. And here it is!"

Defilak pointed to his creation with pride. It was a slim, completely enclosed undersea vehicle made from metallic protodermis and crystalline protodermis. He had obviously used the Takea shark as a model, for his design had the same general shape and fin structure. The cockpit was large enough to seat four, and two large windows afforded a view of the outside. A claw grabber was mounted on the front and two launchers were on either side, designed to fire prototype spheres of solid air. Short protodermis stakes were attached to a gear on the back.

One of the volunteers, a Ta-Matoran named Sarda, looked over the craft. "I've never seen anything like it," he said. "And I sort of hope I never will again. What does it do?"

"It can go down into the black water, explore, and then rise back up to Mahri Nui. You turn a handle inside to make the gear go circle-round and make the ship move, and —"

"Wait a minute," said Gar. "What about the Matoran you built this for? Did he ever use it?"

"Um, well, you see," Defilak replied. "He kind of had second thoughts after he got a look at it. But I promise you it will work!"

"So you've tested it?"

"No."

"You've seen something similar work?"

"Well . . . no."

"Then how can you be so sure?"

Defilak threw his shoulders back proudly and said, "I have enormous trust-faith in my own talent."

Gar frowned. "I think maybe I'll do something safer with my day, like hand-feed hungry sharks."

By the time safe hour came again, Defilak had managed to recruit one more crew member, a Ga-Matoran named Idris. Together they carried

Defilak's craft to the edge of a tidal pool within one of the smaller shelters. They gently placed it in the center of the pool and one by one climbed inside. The interior was cramped and the air smelled stale, but at least it was dry.

Once everyone was in place, Defilak pulled a lever. Water flooded into the empty space between the inner and outer hulls and the craft began to sink underwater. All four Matoran fought down a surge of fear. They were descending into the unknown in a vehicle they felt sure would not be able to withstand an attack by the enemy. But no one suggested turning back.

While Gar turned the crank, Defilak maneuvered the craft through the narrow tunnel and into the open sea. They were perhaps a hundred feet below the edge of the fields of air, and still descending. No Matoran had ever willingly gone any deeper than this.

The world viewed through the crystalline protodermis windows was wondrous. Light-stones mounted on the outside of the craft revealed schools of tiny fish darting about. Strange vegetation coiled around rocks, strands waving gently in the current. Creatures no Matoran had ever even imagined, let alone seen, swam near the craft, then backed off when they realized it was not just some new type of marine life. It was simultaneously stunningly beautiful and incredibly eerie, leaving the Matoran unsure of just how to react to what they saw.

"How far down do you think we'll have to go?" asked Sarda.

"No way to know," said Defilak. "Maybe we will deep-dive all the way to the very bottom of the ocean."

"What if the stories are true?" asked Idris. "You know, the tales about evil beings haunting the seafloor, banished from the light for all time? No one knows if they're dead or alive, and —"

"And no one knows if you're crazy or you just like scaring us all to death," said Sarda. "They're stories, just stories . . . and nothing in a story can hurt you. Right?"

No one chose to answer.

* * *

By the time Kyrehx made it to the Council chamber, no one was there. She thought furiously, *Who would be the best being to tell about this mask?* She was excited about what she had found but also a little fearful, and a growing part of her wanted nothing more than to hand it off to someone else.

Then it hit her. One of her instructors on sea life had made a hobby of carving replicas of Kanohi masks out of stone. If anyone might know just what mask this was, it was he. Kyrehx tucked the mask under her arm and started for the school.

She made it only a few feet before something snagged her foot. Looking down, she saw that a strand of seaweed growing from between two cracks in the rock had wound around her ankle. With a determined yank, she pulled free.

Passing through the Council chamber's air bubble, she began to swim toward her destination. It was slow going. The work crew whose job it was to keep swimways clear of vegetation had evidently not been been very diligent, for the path was choked with greenery. She had to push it aside as she went, not easy when she had only one hand free.

It only grew more difficult as she went on. The seaweed and ocean grass was up over her head now and she could barely see the city through the plant growth. Frustrated, she reached out and tore a stalk of ocean grass out of the ground. The action should have made her feel better, if only in a small way. Instead, she was struck dumb with fear when she heard the grass scream.

Suddenly, the vegetation around her was moving. Weeds were reaching out to grab her arms and legs. Another patch of ocean grass was already shooting up from the spot vacated by the stalk she had torn up. Furiously, she hacked at the growth with her blades, trying to ignore the yells that greeted each blow.

Then she saw a hand reaching for her. It was the armored hand of a Po-Matoran who was standing outside of the plant prison that caged her. She grabbed on and felt herself being pulled through the stubborn weeds. The plants pulled back, not wanting to relinquish their prize. But the strength of the Po-Matoran proved greater, and both Kyrehx and the Kanohi mask came flying out.

The Po-Matoran pointed to the wildly growing plants, puzzled. She signaled to him that he should not think, just swim. It was good advice, for the plants were already reaching for her again.

Together, the two Matoran raced for the nearest building. Once inside the structure's air bubble, they ran inside the shelter and slammed the door behind them.

"What in Mata Nui's name is going on?" demanded the Po-Matoran. "And what's that mask you're carrying?"

"I'm starting to think both questions might have the same answer," Kyrehx answered.

The Po-Matoran, a waterhunter named Dekar, reached out and took the mask. He was no expert on Kanohi, but he could tell this particular mask was very old. At first, he thought it remarkable that something so ancient could be not only intact, but undamaged. Before he could comment on that, though, he noticed the tiniest of hairline cracks along the top edge of the mask.

"You didn't put this on?" he asked.

"No," Kyrehx answered. "And even if I had, you know Matoran can't use mask powers."

"Right. Of course we can't," he said, turning the mask over in his hands. "Where were you taking it?"

"To the school — I thought they would want to — I thought it would be best if it was with someone of learning. Then the plants went crazy, the whole world went crazy, and —"

Dekar walked to the window and looked out at the city. Kyrehx joined him. Everything looked normal. The plants she had fought her way through had receded and were back to their normal height. Nothing was trying to get at her. She breathed a long sigh of relief.

"That was so weird," Kyrehx said, smiling. "Must have been some plant virus or something."

"Must have been," Dekar agreed. He held

out the mask. "Here, this is yours. Take it where you need to."

Instinctively, the Ga-Matoran backed away. Suddenly, the last thing she wanted was to be anywhere near that mask. "Tell you what," she said. "You take it. You saved my life, so you should get the glory of finding a new artifact. Really, it's okay."

Dekar started to protest, but she was already out the door and swimming rapidly away. He watched her go, then looked back at the Kanohi. He couldn't see any sense in her behavior. Then again, he had never understood Ga-Matoran very well anyway.

He tucked the artifact in his pack. There would be time enough to take it to the school later on. He had hunting to do.

After all, he reasoned, *it's just another mask. Not like one mask is going to change anything down here.*

The squid swam swiftly through an underwater cavern. It passed many of its species, most of them busy feeding on marine life unwise enough to come too close. Unlike some similar Rahi species, this type of squid did not have to rely on beaked mouths to feed. The suckers on their tentacles drained the life force from any being they touched. Their speed and ruthless efficiency made them creatures to be dreaded by even the great sharks.

Feeding was the last thing on this creature's mind right now, however. Its instinct led it right to the deepest part of the cave, where its master waited.

Three eyes gleamed in the back of the cavern, but only two darted toward the squid as it entered. The master's third eye had been ruined in battle years ago. This would normally have meant he was vulnerable to attacks from his blind side, and in a place like this, that would quickly spell death. Fortunately, the small tentacles on the back of his head acted as a sensory apparatus and made up for the loss of the eye.

The master's great tentacle reached out and brushed against the squid. In that instant, information was exchanged from being to being. All that the squid had seen now resided in its master's memory as well.

A mask of such great power that this beast could sense its energies from far away . . . a mask active even when not being worn, thought the tentacled cave dweller. *It could not be — and then again, why not? Perhaps the universe has followed us all into the abyss.*

He broke contact with the squid and dismissed it. What would need to be done could not be accomplished by mere Rahi. It was time to seek out the others. It was time to hunt again.

Kalmah rose from his throne of bones and swam toward the cave mouth and the open sea beyond. After so many millennia in this place, salvation had arrived in the form of a Kanohi mask. And, like all sources of power, it would belong to those with the strength to seize it.

The empire of the Barraki was about to live again.

THREE

"How do we know?" asked Sarda abruptly.

"How do we know what?" Defilak replied.

"How do we know there's anything down here but fish? All we know is something has been attacking our people for centuries. What makes you think it's down here in the black water?"

"Well, this area has never been explored, for one thing."

Idris laughed softly. "You could say that about a lot of places, Defilak. The pillars of salt . . . the high mountains . . . most of the area around the city is still a mystery, you know."

"Not surprising," said Defilak. "Remember the history. Some trouble-bad happened, and we and our city wound up beneath the sea. If the impact hadn't disturbed the fields of air, setting free scores of small bubbles, we would all have suffocated. Then everyone started to quick-change . . . it was only staying inside the air bubbles that stopped that."

Gar remembered. Dozens and dozens of Matoran had died when Mahri Nui sank. They still didn't know why the disaster had happened or even exactly where they had been before. But Defilak was right — if they had not discovered the products of the fields of air within moments after sinking, they would have died, or mutated, or maybe something worse.

There's something evil about these waters, he thought. *It's like the sea here is not just filled with living things but is a living thing itself . . . living, and hungry.*

The craft lurched to the left. Then it did so a second time, more violently, this time clearly from an impact. "Watch the rocks," Gar said.

"I am close-watching them!" snapped Defilak. "We're not hitting anything. Something's hitting us!"

"I saw it!" cried Idris. "Just for a second . . . something flashed by."

Gar pressed his mask against the crystal-line windows of the cockpit. The placid schools of fish were gone. They knew by instinct when it was time to hide again because predators were on the prowl. It was by watching them that the Matoran of Mahri Nui had learned there was a safe hour. It began when the prey fish came out in great numbers, and ended when they fled back to their hiding places in reefs and between rocks.

Now today's safe hour was over. The hunt-ers were back, and one of them was hunting the Matorans' vehicle.

"Sarda, quick-work that crank," Defilak ordered. "We need more speed. Idris, hands on the lever. Be ready to throw it and send us back up."

Something struck the craft on the right side, then on the left. Then the impact came from behind, sending the fragile vehicle rocketing for-ward. After that, all the jarring came from the rear of the craft being struck, almost as if it was being shoved toward some unknown destination.

"What's doing this?" said Idris, panic in her voice. "Why doesn't it show itself?"

"They don't want us to clear-see them," said Defilak. "They're trying to scare us."

"It's working," muttered Sarda.

The impacts stopped. The four Matoran sat very still, listening for any sound, watching for any glimpse of their attacker through the crystal. Sarda started to speak, but Defilak raised a finger to his mask to order silence. Then he gestured for Sarda to stop turning the crank that kept the vessel moving forward.

The craft began to slowly sink toward the bottom of the sea. Both Idris and Sarda looked at Defilak, wondering what he had in mind. The truth was that the Le-Matoran was not certain himself. He was gambling that perhaps whatever was stalking them relied on hearing more than sight, so a lack of sound might frustrate its pursuit.

There was another impact, more severe than any before, this time on the bottom of the craft. Whatever was out there didn't want them to go any lower. It was trying to nudge them back up.

A silver scale flashed past the cockpit windows. The craft shook from another impact, then six, then ten, rocking it every which way. Now the attackers were visible, circling the vehicle, getting ready for the kill.

They were Takea sharks, dozens of them, dead eyes fixed on the craft and sharp teeth ready to savage the metal to get at their prey. But what was really disturbing was the figure that hovered beyond them — the one with the Takea shark's fin and features and dagger-like teeth . . . and two arms, and two legs, and weapons no marine Rahi could have forged.

Defilak suddenly had the sickening feeling that they had found what they came down looking for. Now they just had to survive their success.

For as many years as he could remember clearly, Dekar had loved to hunt. It was a chance to get away from the stifling confines of Mahri Nui and see a little bit of the watery world that surrounded the city. Although he was doing important work, bringing in prey fish and keeping predators away from the borders, this was also his private time. It was Dekar's chance to be alone with his thoughts.

Today his thoughts were centered on the Kanohi mask he carried in his pack. Where had it come from? What was its power? Was there really some connection between it and what had happened to that Ga-Matoran Kyrehx, as she seemed to suggest? Or had nature simply gone a little crazy for a while?

Well, one thing he was certain of — he did not feel any different since taking the mask. No vegetation had reached out to grab him, and the fish were certainly not swimming for his net. She had probably just been on sentry duty for too long, or maybe she let her personal air bubble get a little too thin.

A movement caught Dekar's eye. He directed his lightstone toward the motion, revealing what looked like a ribbon of darkness in the water. It traveled in a strange, sidewinding manner characteristic of only one sea creature he knew of: a venom eel.

Venom eels were distant relations of the lava eels that were usually found near volcanoes on the surface. But while lava eels' most dangerous talent was increasing their outer temperature to metal-melting levels, venom eels relied on a quick-acting poison delivered through their sharp fangs. Unlike most sea creatures, they did not rely on their sense of smell but primarily on their eyesight and, to a lesser extent, their hearing. They were attracted to any bit of light or motion.

The appearance of a venom eel in open water puzzled Dekar. The creatures generally remained camouflaged and waited for prey to come to them. To help themselves stay hidden, their metallic hide had no scales that might reflect a stray beam of light. Rather, it was solid black and covered in slime. Though certainly a threat to Matoran if annoyed or attacked, they rarely sought out Mahri Nui's residents. This was good news, for their frightening appearance alone was enough to freeze most opponents.

Fighting a venom eel was not something Dekar looked forward to. But allowing one to venture too close to the city would put other waterhunters and sentries at risk. He swam toward the creature, determined to drive it off.

Right away, he knew something was wrong. The venom eel was even more aggressive than normal for its species. Twice it shot forward and tried to bite Dekar, narrowly missing both times. He thrust his spear at it, not really aiming to hurt but more to scare. The eel latched on to Dekar's weapon with its jaws, trying to wrench it free from his grasp.

This was deadly serious. Dekar now believed the venom eel was sick, mad, or maybe both. Allowing such a creature free rein so close to Mahri Nui would be disastrous. The venom eel would have to be killed for the safety of all.

The eel turned, preparing to strike again, briefly exposing its flank. Dekar thrust with his spear, piercing the creature's armor and reaching the soft tissue beneath. Convinced it was a fatal strike, he pulled the spear out and backed away from the creature.

But the venom eel was not mortally wounded. Before Dekar's eyes, the wound made by the spear instantly healed.

Dekar tried again, and for a second time he managed to strike what should have been a final blow. Instead, the damage was erased in seconds. The Po-Matoran could practically see the creature's muscle regenerating.

Dekar was a brave Matoran, one who had fought many sea Rahi over the centuries and valiantly defended his city. So, faced with a creature that apparently could not be killed, he could be forgiven if the impulse to flee overcame him. Dekar looked back only once as he swam for Mahri Nui, and what he saw made him race all the faster for a safe haven.

It resembled a black cloud moving rapidly through the water, headed straight for the city.

Viewed a little closer, it might seem like a huge patch of vegetation that had somehow come detached from the seafloor and now floated through the ocean.

But the mass of writhing shapes was not made of smoke and dust, nor were the tendrils that slashed through the water with such purpose mere strands of seaweed. No, this bizarre sight was not some harmless underwater phenomenon.

It was venom eels — thousands of them — massed for an attack on Mahri Nui.

From her sentry post, Kyrehx saw them, too. She didn't pause to wonder why or how the creatures were moving on the city. After what she had just been through, she wasn't in the mood to question anything. She just grabbed the shell horn and blew into it, sounding the alarm signal.

Matoran poured out of their homes and workplaces, already loading their launchers with spheres of solidified air. These were an invention of an eccentric Le-Matoran scientist inspired by the hydruha's means of defense. He originally intended them as a means of transport (the idea being that Matoran could actually ride on the bubbles at a much faster rate than even a Ga-Matoran could swim). Unfortunately, in his first test of the system, he had ridden one of the spheres straight into the powerful arms of a Tarakava and was never seen again. The concept of solid air spheres for transportation was scrapped and the invention was turned into a weapon.

The theory was simple. The air spheres were fired from a shoulder-mounted launcher. When they struck their target, they "shattered" and went back to being a gas. Though harmless against Matoran or other air-breathing species, the weapon was devastating to water breathers, for whom air was a toxic substance.

As the city's defenders took their places, Kyrehx moved to her assigned position. She had one of the most important jobs, helping to guard the hydruka pens. If those beasts were lost, the Matoran would have no reliable way to harvest the fields of air.

A red hydruka skittered backward at her approach. "Relax, Thulox," she said to the creature. "Everything will be all right. It's just some Rahi who are headed in the wrong direction. Maybe an undersea storm confused them."

Even as she said the words, she realized they couldn't be true. A storm powerful enough to drive that many venom eels out of their lairs would have devastated Mahri Nui already. Something else was at work here.

She climbed onto some rocks overlooking the pens. In the distance, she could see the rest of her squad swimming to join her. They were waving and pointing, as if trying to tell her where they would take up position. She pointed to the left, indicating she would swing around to the far side of the rocks where she could better defend the outer fields.

She realized too late that her friends were not signaling her about strategy. They were trying to warn her about something looming behind her. Suddenly a huge claw snapped shut around her and she was being dragged through the water toward

Mahri Rock. She kicked and flailed, but it did no good. Whatever had her was not letting go. By the time the rest of her squad reached the fields of air, she was nowhere to be seen.

Carapar glanced at the squirming Ga-Matoran in his grasp. It seemed hard to believe that such a weak little thing might have had her hands on any object powerful enough to matter. But Kalmah had sworn this one was seen with the mask, and if she didn't have it, she would know where it was.

It was Carapar's job to find out what she knew. And if she didn't survive the experience . . . well, the sea was a harsh place, after all.

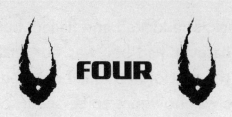

FOUR

The sound of tearing metal signaled the beginning of the end. It was followed by the sight of water gushing into the small craft from a gap in the side. The Takea sharks were no longer content just to pummel the Matoran's vehicle — now they were trying to devour it.

Defilak didn't hesitate. "Idris, throw that lever!"

The sharks struck again, this time ripping huge holes in the craft's hull. Idris pulled the lever that should have sent the vehicle shooting back up toward Mahri Nui. An explosion of air sent the water hurtling out of the space between the inner and outer hull, but there was already so much water leaking in that the craft couldn't rise. In fact, it was doing the opposite.

"We're sinking!" Gar shouted.

"We're snacks," Sarda replied, pointing to the Takea sharks.

"Get ready to fast-swim," said Defilak. "Make sure your launchers are loaded. If you make it back to the city, let them know what we found. There's something dark-strange about all this."

"We won't stand a chance!" Sarda answered. "Those Takea sharks will rip us to pieces in seconds!"

As if in agreement, the sharks tore more holes in the sides of the craft. The Matoran were now hip-deep in water and it was rising fast. Defilak didn't bother answering Sarda, because the Ta-Matoran was right. None of them was going to make it out of this. But sharks didn't accept surrenders, so they were going to have to try.

Another attack tore open a gap big enough for a Matoran to slip through. "Go!" Defilak shouted. The four shot out of the hole and into a sea teeming with Takea sharks. Expecting at any moment to feel jaws clamping on their legs, they swam furiously up toward the city.

Amazingly, the sharks did not attack. Instead, they moved aside, creating a path for the Matoran. The swimmers made it a few yards unscathed. They almost started to hope that they might make it to Mahri Nui after all.

Then the hunters of the sea closed in. Defilak looked around to see that he and his friends were surrounded. Still, none of the sharks were attacking. It seemed as if they just wanted to cut off the Matoran's flight.

Defilak glanced below. The craft had been fatally breached. As he watched, it sank down into the black water and was gone from sight.

The ring of sharks tightened. Then the creatures formed a line and began to herd the Matoran down into the depths. And all the while, the strange shark-like being watched, predatory eyes fixed on his captives.

The four Matoran were taken to an undersea cave and forced inside a small bubble of air. The school of sharks then withdrew, although a few remained visible swimming back and forth in front of the cave mouth. Only the shark-like being stayed in the cave with the Matoran. He looked them over one by one. Defilak wasn't sure if he was sizing them up as foes or as possible future meals. *Then again, maybe it's both,* the Matoran thought.

Then, to the Matoran's shock, the strange creature spoke. "I am Pridak," he said. "I bid you welcome to my domain."

"You have an ever-odd way of sending an invitation," Defilak answered.

Pridak smiled, revealing rows of vicious teeth. "You invaded my world, Matoran. By right, I could have had you killed. Instead, I offer you my hospitality." When the Matoran did not respond, he added, "The proper words are 'thank you.'"

"Does your hospitality usually include tearing watercraft to bits?" Defilak snapped.

"My pets get enthusiastic," Pridak replied coldly. "Beware, Matoran, or you may find out firsthand just *how* enthusiastic they can be."

"Enough," said Defilak. "You must want something, Pridak. Why not tell us what it is? We went below seeking peace, not war."

"Peace?" Pridak spat. "You and your kind are weaker than even I believed. But very well — as you have no doubt noticed, the air in your bubble is growing thinner by the moment, so we will waste no more time. I want the mask. It wasn't in your absurd craft. Where is it?"

The four Matoran looked at each other, confused. Then Sarda said, "We don't know what you're talking about. What mask?"

Pridak moved with impossible speed. Before the Matoran could even think of resistance, he reached in and yanked Sarda out of the bubble. Then he swam a few yards toward the cave mouth and hurled the protesting Matoran out of the cave and into the open ocean. Defilak could see the Takea sharks reacting to the new presence in their midst. The whole incident had happened in a matter of seconds.

"Will he live?" Pridak asked. "Will he die? Do I care? Not at all. But you do, Matoran. You have one minute to tell me what I want to know. Then the Ga-Matoran joins her friend."

Not far away, another Ga-Matoran had troubles of her own.

Kyrehx had been brought to a sea cave, but there was no air bubble waiting there for her. Worse, her personal supply of air was rapidly dwindling. The crab-like being, who said his name was Carapar, dragged her down a long tunnel that looked as if it might once have belonged to undersea worms. At the other end of it waited another strange creature.

At first, Kyrehx thought the bizarre being might be dead. He sat motionless in the cave, red eyes staring straight ahead, looking for all the world like he had never moved in the last year. In comparison to Carapar, he seemed physically weak, but there was a sense of menace about him that sent a chill through the Ga-Matoran.

Suddenly, he moved. The action startled Kyrehx and she screamed — and immediately regretted it, for it used up more of her air. The creature in the cave regarded her as he would a not very appetizing meal. Then he glanced at the crablike being who had brought her here.

"Very well, Carapar, you are finished."

Carapar shook his head, as if he were awakening from a nap. He looked around the cave in confusion. Then his eyes settled on the cavern's resident and comprehension dawned on his features.

"Takadox!" he bellowed. "I thought I told you not to do that anymore! I ought to feed you to the keras crabs and be done with it!"

Takadox smiled. "Calm yourself, Carapar. You don't want to get so excited."

"Calm . . . myself," Carapar repeated, slowly. "I don't want to . . . don't . . . no!" The crab being threw up one of his claws to block his eyes. "Not again, Takadox. I won't warn you again."

The hideous creature laughed at Carapar's discomfort. Then he turned his attention to Kyrehx. "Little Matoran, lost and alone," he crooned softly. "So far away from home. But we will be your friends now, Carapar and I."

Kyrehx felt Takadox's eyes boring into hers. She was terrified initially, but then the fear eased. What he was saying made sense. She was lost and she had no idea how to get back to Mahri Nui. . . . Wasn't she lucky she had landed among such good friends? She felt warm and open, as if she had known Takadox and Carapar all her life.

"Friends have no secrets from each other, do they?" Takadox continued, half speaking and half singing. "You wouldn't want to keep any secrets from us, would you?"

"No . . ." Kyrehx replied, and it was true. She couldn't even conceive of hiding anything from her two good friends.

Takadox glanced at Carapar. "You see? It's so much more effective than your bludgeoning approach to things. As soon as she looked into my eyes, the poor Matoran was lost. Now she will tell us whatever she knows."

Carapar looked at the Ga-Matoran. Yes, she was in a trance, similar to the ones he had seen Takadox induce in so many others. Millennia before, Takadox had boasted of having the most loyal of all the six armies, for each and every one of his soldiers had been hypnotized into complete obedience. He was right; it was an effective tool for interrogation. But the idea still made Carapar a little sick. "Just get on with it," he muttered.

Takadox nodded and turned back to Kyrehx. "Now, little one, why don't you tell us all about that mask you found?"

In halting tones, the Ga-Matoran related everything that had happened since she had spotted the mask floating in the water. Takadox made her go back and describe how it looked in great detail. When she was done, he gave a low whistle.

"Then the legends are true," he said, in a voice so soft Carapar had to strain to hear. "There is a Mask of Life. It's the key to our prison — and all that stands between us and freedom is a band of puny little Matoran."

Takadox turned to his partner, who by reflex covered his eyes. "As much as it may grieve me to admit this, the others have to know what we have learned. We began this journey together, and we must end it the same way."

"Why?" asked Carapar. There was no sarcasm or bitterness in his voice. It was just a simple question from a being that excelled at them. And Takadox, for the life of him, could not think of a good answer, so he chose to ignore the question.

"Gather the others. We must make contact with the Matoran and convince them to give us the mask."

Carapar chuckled, a sound like fish bones being ground between shark teeth. "A little late for that — Ehlek and his venom eels are 'making contact' right now. Before another safe hour rolls around, there won't be anything left alive in that city."

"No!" Takadox shouted, actually rising to his feet for the first time in ages. "The mask will be lost . . . or worse! Go to the city now, Carapar, and stop his ridiculous attack before he ruins everything!"

"Pridak won't like that," Carapar replied. "You know how 'the shark' feels about Matoran."

"Let me deal with Pridak," said Takadox. "You do what I asked."

The crab being gestured toward the still entranced Ga-Matoran. "What about her?"

An expression of contempt flitted across Takadox's features, giving Carapar hope that an exquisite death would be in the Matoran's future. Then Takadox surprised him by saying, "Take her back to her city and set her free."

"What?" Carapar shouted. "Have you gone soft-shelled?"

"Do you remember that small island on the western edge of your realm? The one that held out the longest against your armies?"

"Sure. What about it?"

"How did you finally conquer it?"

Carapar thought back. There had been so many conquests over the centuries, it was hard to keep them straight. "I . . . let me think . . . yes, I offered peace negotiations and presented them with a bounty of food as a gesture of friendship."

"And the food was tainted, wasn't it? The whole population was sick within hours and able to offer no resistance, isn't that so?"

Carapar smiled broadly. Yes, that had been a glorious victory, although the condition of the enemy did cut way down on the joyful sound of screaming.

"Then you see my point," Takadox finished. "Sometimes, the most effective first blow in a battle comes wrapped as a gift."

Dekar was angrier than he had ever been. He had made it back to Mahri Nui barely ahead of his pursuers. The defenders had given him command of one of the largest air launchers. With perfect aim and amazing precision, he had fired air spheres at the approaching eels to drive them back — and it had done no good at all.

Each time, the spheres struck on target. The air turned from solid to gas. The eels faltered as the substance, so toxic to them, took effect. Then they would seem to shake it off and keep on coming toward the city. Dekar had never seen anything like it before, but he was pretty certain he understood why it was happening.

The mask, he thought grimly. *I don't know how or why, but it won't let anything die. When I speared the eel, it healed the wound. When I try to poison them with air, it dispels the gas. Kyrehx was telling the truth — it must have been responsible for the plant growth, too. It's the only answer that makes sense.*

There was only one thing to do. If he gave the mask to another Matoran, it would just transfer its power to its new owner — and maybe do something worse than it had up to now. No, passing the problem on to someone else would just be cowardice.

Dekar took the Kanohi mask out of his pack. *Sorry, whatever you are, but you've left me no choice,* he thought. *If I can't get rid of you . . . I'll have to destroy you.*

FIVE

"We . . . we destroyed it!" said Defilak. "There is no mask, not anymore."

Pridak did not loosen his grip on Idris, but he did not drag her out of the air bubble either. His dead eyes regarded Defilak carefully, looking for any sign of deception. But the Le-Matoran met his gaze, and the Onu-Matoran behind him was nodding his agreement.

"Is this true?" Pridak growled at Idris. She was too frightened to even try to answer.

"She doesn't true-know," said Defilak. "She wasn't there. Gar and I decided."

Pridak let Idris go and swam toward where Defilak stood. "Why would you destroy anything that might help you survive down here?" he asked, suspicious.

Defilak shrugged. "Help us survive, how? Matoran can't use mask powers. We have extra masks if one of ours gets far-lost or broken. All we could do with another Kanohi is hang it up as a piece of art. We don't have room in our city for anything that isn't useful."

Pridak reached into the bubble and passed the edge of his weapon beneath Defilak's chin. "Before you said you didn't know of any mask, . . . now you say you destroyed it. Why deny knowing of it if it was already gone? What are you hiding, little meal?"

"We should tell you the business of Mahri Nui?" Defilak answered, defiantly. "You attack us, you imprison us — what right do you have to do any of this?"

"What right?" Pridak replied, his tone as cold as the water he swam in. "The right of a ruler. The right of a conqueror. The right of a Barraki."

A memory suddenly exploded in Defilak's mind. He saw himself on dry land, sitting at the feet of a Turaga. The Turaga was telling a story about six powerful beings called Barraki and how they dared the impossible . . . and paid the price for it. He could hear only brief snatches of what the Turaga was saying, but it was enough to tell him that this shark-thing in front of him could not be a Barraki.

Before he could stop himself, Defilak said, "You're a fraud. Barraki were not creatures of the water-depths. They were warlords of the surface world."

Pridak reached into the bubble and dragged Defilak out. Only the fact that his personal air bubble was still in existence, if razor thin, kept the Matoran from drowning immediately. "Come with me," said Pridak. "I want to tell you a tale, morsel. I hate to see anyone die ignorant."

Pridak brought Defilak up to the top of the salt mountains that overlooked Mahri Nui. The Matoran's eyes widened with shock at the sight of his friends fighting for their lives against an army of venom eels. Pridak laughed at his obvious concern.

"They will be the lucky ones," he said, gesturing toward the defenders. "They will be free of the Pit in the only way you can be, through nonexistence. And they will die in battle — glorious, all-consuming battle — a privilege not granted to the Barraki. No, we were condemned to a living death."

"You keep calling yourself by that name," Defilak said. "But the Barraki were said to be titan-masters — rulers who dominated wherever they went and left lesser beings in awe. They weren't . . . um . . ."

Pridak brought his face up close to Defilak's mask and hissed, "Say it! Go on, morsel, say what you are thinking. The Barraki were not monstrous creatures of the sea, skulking in caves or lurking in the black water out of sight of 'civilized' Matoran."

Defilak didn't answer, preferring to go on living for at least another minute. Pridak slowly backed away, his rage subsiding. The Barraki gestured toward the battle with a clawed hand and whispered, "Isn't it glorious? The fighting . . . the shouting . . . the desperate struggle to survive . . ."

"No," said Defilak. "It's horrible."

"Ah, well," Pridak replied, shrugging. "As I

always say, good taste is in the jaws of the devourer. But I promised you a tale before you died, didn't I? There was a time when I did not look as I do now, or have to subsist on the bottom feeders of this cursed sea. I was a conqueror, and undisputed leader of the League of the Six Kingdoms."

The name stirred another memory in Defilak's mind. Yes, his Turaga had mentioned the League in the tales told around the night fires. Something about the alliance of rulers falling from its exalted position and coming to a very bad end . . .

"We rose up against the Great Spirit Mata Nui," Pridak said, sounding as if it had just happened yesterday. "And we were crushed for our efforts, our armies shattered, our realms no doubt ground to dust. Makuta would have taken our lives — the only decent thing he could do — had not the creature Botar intervened. He brought us to a place of darkness and misery, and there we stayed for thousands and thousands of years.

Pridak snatched a passing fish out of the

water. He eyed it as if it were a potential meal. Then, dissatisfied with its size, he threw it to some Takea sharks that were circling overhead. "We survived, and we planned," he said. "And we learned to hate with an all-consuming fury — hate Mata Nui, hate Makuta, hate everything that could walk on dry land and breathe the air, as we no longer could."

The sharks had devoured the fish and now moved on in search of other prey. They split up, herding smaller fish into a tight ball before mounting their ferocious, and very successful, attack. The sight chilled Defilak.

"Then came our deliverance," Pridak continued. "A great earthquake shook our world. The walls of our prison ruptured and we were able to swim out into the black water. And there we . . . changed . . . into what you see before you, and worse. Working together, the six of us built a realm here, a first stepping-stone toward greater conquests. Then your city, Matoran, came crashing down through the water and obliterated all that we had created. Fate, it seemed, had struck at us again."

Defilak shook his head, just trying to take it all in. The sinking of Mahri Nui had been so traumatic that none of the Matoran had a very clear memory of it. Certainly they had never realized that their city had destroyed another. He could well understand why that must have seemed to the Barraki like the wrath of the Great Spirit unleashed.

"And now this mask," said Pridak, slowly. "I don't know what it is, or why it is so important, but it is a new element. Perhaps it is the weapon we have waited for. You can tell me where it is — or you can spend the last moments of your life watching your people and your city die."

Defilak looked from Pridak to Mahri Nui. Then he made his decision.

"All right. I'll give you the mask," the Matoran lied. "But I can't quick-tell you where it is — I'll have to show you."

* * *

Carapar swam toward Mahri Nui, Kyrehx in tow. The Ga-Matoran's air bubble was almost gone and her breathing was shallow. In a few more moments, she would be dead from suffocation and of no use as a "gift" to the Matoran. With this in mind, Carapar brought her to the edge of a field of airweed, taking care to stay far away from the plants himself. Like the other creatures of the Pit, air was toxic to him.

Kyrehx groped through the plants until she disturbed one enough that it unleashed a bubble of air. She thrust her head inside it and took a long breath. Then she turned to Carapar, puzzled. "Why did you save me?"

"'Cause if I kill you, I have to explain it to Takadox," the Barraki answered. "And I hate explaining things to Takadox."

Carapar dragged her back out of the field. Pointing toward the city, he said, "Go home, while it's still there. Make your peace with Mahri Nui. You and yours are about to be swept away with the tide."

Kyrehx couldn't respond without exhaling,

so she turned and swam as fast as she could for Mahri Nui. Carapar watched her go. Then he looked up and spotted his fellow Barraki, Ehlek, swimming amidst a swarm of venom eels. He moved to intercept.

Kalmah moved slowly through the water, his two good eyes searching the dark brown sands for any sign of life. He had no doubt the being he sought was hidden somewhere beneath the soil, but just where was a mystery. Caution was essential, too, for the appetite of his target was legendary and anything passing overhead was fair game.

He paused. Was that a pair of gems glittering in the seabed? And were those the bones of some long-dead creature sticking out of the sand nearby? No, he realized. Those were the eyes and head spikes of Mantax as he waited, buried in the earth, for his next meal to pass by.

Kalmah decided the indirect approach was best. He had no desire to wind up with some part of his anatomy trapped in Mantax's pincer.

He sent his long tentacle snaking into the sand until it was close to his fellow Barraki. Then Kalmah swiftly wrapped it around Mantax's waist and yanked the surprised creature out of his hiding place.

"What are you doing?" Mantax demanded, clearly uncomfortable with being exposed. "There might have been food coming!"

"All right. I'll just tell Pridak that you are too busy dining to join us," Kalmah answered. "Maybe he will send Carapar to come get you."

Mantax stiffened. He was more than willing to challenge Pridak or anything else under the sea, but his occasional clashes with Carapar had not ended well. Carapar had two pincers to his one, and a longer reach on top of that.

"Very well," Mantax grumbled. "The first time I followed Pridak, I got condemned to the Pit. The second time, my dwelling got crushed by a Matoran city. How will he destroy my life this time, I wonder?"

"Not destroy," Kalmah said, gesturing with

his tentacle toward the sea caves beyond. "Far from it, in fact. Look."

Mantax wrestled free of Kalmah's grip and focused his attention on the caves. A lone Po-Matoran was swimming toward one of the natural shelters, a Kanohi mask in his hands. Intrigued, the two Barraki took off in pursuit.

Dekar had a plan. First, he would get this mask as far from the city as he safely could, so that there was no chance another Matoran would stumble on him and take it. Once he was in one of the caves, he would smash the mask to pieces. Mahri Nui would be better off without something so dangerous and unpredictable.

He looked over his shoulder to see if any of the other Matoran had followed him. That was when he spotted Mantax and Kalmah closing in. They obviously weren't swimming over to ask directions. Dekar began kicking furiously in an effort to put some distance between him and the sea creatures.

He had managed to gain perhaps a yard or two on them when his lungs began to burn. His air bubble was dangerously thin and about to be extinguished, and he was way too far from the nearest field of airweed to take refuge there. Dekar figured he would be able to hold his breath for two or three minutes, and then it would be over.

Then his eyes alighted on something very curious. A small air bubble was emerging from a crack in the Kanohi mask he held. It drifted toward Dekar and merged with his bubble. Another and another followed, slowly but surely strengthening the cone of air around the Matoran. If he'd had the time, Dekar would have pondered just how miraculous an event this was — a mask that could create air! — but the strange sea creatures were drawing closer again.

Dekar ducked into a cave. He had perhaps a few seconds before his pursuers found him. The air from the mask had bought him time and made him realize how valuable the Kanohi could be to his people. But he was also smart enough to know he would never be able to keep it from the monsters that were chasing him. Even if he hid it, they would find it. And if it could create air, what else might it do? What would it do in the wrong hands?

No, Dekar thought, *I have to stand firm. I have to destroy it before it's too late.*

He put the Kanohi mask down on the cave floor, picked up a rock, and prepared to strike. With luck, one, maybe two, solid blows would be enough to shatter it. *After all, it's cracked already,* he reasoned.

Outside, Mantax and Kalmah reached the cave mouth. They spotted Dekar's arm falling as it brought a rock down toward the mask. It was too late to stop the Matoran — even Kalmah's tentacle would not reach that far.

But what all present had forgotten, or did not know, was that this was no ordinary Kanohi mask. This was the Mask of Life. Forged over 100,000 years ago by the Great Beings who created the universe, it was set apart from every mask that had been or ever would be crafted. It could think, it could feel . . . and as both Matoran and Barraki learned to their shock, when threatened, it could strike back.

SIX

Carapar knew that the words "stop killing everything" would sound to Ehlek like a foreign language. Nervous by nature as "the Eel" might be, he was still the only one of the Barraki who called the ocean floor home. He felt a special hatred for the Matoran for invading his domain and for killing so many sea predators with their air shooters. The existence of this mysterious "Mask of Life" was just an excuse for him to take revenge.

Still, Carapar would have to make the effort, and he had assembled an army of keras crabs to back him up. Keras were normally fairly placid and gentle creatures, but the waters of the Pit had long ago changed them to aggressive, violent beasts. Carapar had split his forces in two. Half followed him to confront Ehlek and his venom eels, and half were sent to inhabit the fields of air.

"Takadox says stop," he shouted.

Ehlek's response was to give off an electric shock — generally, his response to everything. Carapar was already braced for the pain, but it still stung. He grabbed Ehlek in one of his pincers and squeezed until his fellow Barraki screamed.

"If I so much as see a spark, I'll cut you in half," Carapar snarled.

"What do you want?" Ehlek screeched. "I've done nothing to you!"

"It's what you're doing to them that matters," Carapar answered, gesturing with his free pincer to Mahri Nui. "Takadox says stop. He doesn't want them slaughtered . . . yet. Says they have something we want."

"Yes," Ehlek responded. "Lives. Breath. Futures. All of which I am going to take from —"

Carapar squeezed harder until he heard something crack. "What did I say? Did I say, 'Ehlek, go ahead?' I didn't hear myself say that."

To Ehlek's credit, he wasn't about to give

in. "You said . . . not to kill . . . our enemies. Water . . . has rotted . . . your brain. . . ."

Carapar's features darkened and for a moment he considered how nice Ehlek's head would look mounted on a wall. Then the moment passed and he actually began to laugh. "Despite your bad nerves, you always did have guts," he said. "Don't make me spill them out into the sea, okay?"

After a few seconds, Ehlek nodded. Carapar released him. Once he had checked to make sure he was still in one hideous piece, Ehlek signaled his army of eels to halt their attack. "Now what?" he asked.

"Now this," Carapar answered, swimming toward Mahri Nui. He easily dodged a flurry of air spheres, then came to a halt in front of the launcher. The Matoran were frantically reloading. Smiling, Carapar reached into the air bubble, grabbed the launcher and crumpled it into scrap.

"My army is in your air fields," he said. "See? And they stay there until we get the Mask of Life."

The Matoran gunner stared up at Carapar, defiant. "Even if I knew what that was, I wouldn't give it to you . . . whatever you are."

"Crabs get awful hungry sometimes," the Barraki answered. "Awful hungry. They'll eat just about anything that won't eat them first. Ever see a crab eat? First they take their prey in their pincers, then they rip it apart. . . . Pretty gruesome until you get used to it . . . only it's something you never get used to."

The Matoran tried to appear brave in the face of this veiled threat, but the slightest tremble in his frame betrayed him. Carapar leaned in close to the bubble and said, "So, why don't you be a good little future meal and go tell whoever runs this place to hand over the mask? Go ahead. We'll wait."

Glancing toward the fields, the Matoran could imagine the keras ripping and tearing their way through the airweeds. That would destroy any hope Mahri Nui's inhabitants had for survival in this watery realm. He had to make a decision — but what to do?

Then the decision was suddenly taken out of his hands. He looked up, past Carapar, past Ehlek and his legions, toward a massive shape cutting through the water like a juggernaut. He looked and he wished he had not seen.

Gar kicked the stone wall of the cave and cursed. Then, realizing his behavior was just making Idris more nervous, he said, "Sorry. It's all this waiting."

Idris nodded, her eyes never leaving the cave mouth and the sharks beyond. "I know. Do you think Defilak is ever coming back? Or did he end up like poor Sarda?"

Gar didn't answer her directly. There was no point in dwelling on things they couldn't control. They both had at least a little bit of air left in their bubbles. If they made a break for it, maybe one would be lucky enough to make it back to the city. Anything was better than this.

"We're not going to hang around and find out," the Onu-Matoran said. "Get ready to swim. When we reach open water, I'll try to hold off the sharks long enough for you to get a head start toward the city. Don't turn back, and don't stop for anything — understand?"

Idris turned to look at him. She said nothing, but her eyes reflected what she was feeling. She knew Gar was quite possibly about to sacrifice his life for her, a Ga-Matoran he barely knew. She was also quite certain neither one of them was going to live through this escape attempt. *But Matoran will survive,* she said to herself. *Mahri Nui will survive. As long as there are Gars in the universe, somehow we will find a way.*

"I'm ready," she replied.

"All right, we go on three. One . . ."

A violent impact shook the cave. Idris could see the Takea sharks outside being hurled about like strands of seaweed in a whirlpool. She didn't know if this was something natural — an undersea quake, perhaps — or another attack, but it was their chance.

"Three!" she shouted, rocketing out of the air bubble and heading for the cave mouth, with Gar right behind.

Outside, the sharks were doing something no Matoran had ever seen before — they were fleeing for their lives. A glance upward told Idris and Gar the reason. The sharks had good sense, it seemed, and would survive to see another day. Unless they got moving — fast — the same would not be said for the two Matoran.

Defilak had no idea where he was going.

He had lied to Pridak to buy time to think. There had to be a way to escape and free Gar and Idris. But first he had to ditch this Barraki, and as anyone who has ever tried to evade a shark knew, this would not be easy.

"I think we quick-hid it there," he said, pointing toward the lowlands. "Under a clump of seaweed . . . funny, they all look alike now. I'm sure that's happened to you — you know, you're all set to slash-kill some innocent Matoran, but then we all start to look alike to you."

Pridak ignored the jibe. He was more concerned with a slight shift in the feel of the ocean's energy, something only one with his enhanced senses would pick up on. Something wasn't right, but he could not put his fin on what. It unsettled him.

"Hurry up," he growled. "You are stalling, morsel — keep doing it and you'll be returning to Mahri Nui in pieces."

"It's down there. I'm sure of it," Defilak said. Then he added, "I think."

When Pridak didn't answer, Defilak turned to look at him. The Barraki was hovering in the water, his eyes fixed on nothing, as if he were waiting for something to happen. The Le-Matoran scanned the surrounding water. Prey fish and predators alike were scrambling for cover, as if they sensed impending doom.

"The last time this happened," Pridak muttered, "your city sank beneath the waves, crushing everything in its path. What new disaster are you Matoran unleashing now?"

Then both Barraki and Matoran saw. Being residents of the ocean's lower depths, both were used to the frigid temperatures of the water. Physical cold was something one learned to live with in order to survive here, and eventually, it could even be ignored.

But the sight that greeted Pridak and Defilak's eyes was one to freeze the spirit. It was death given form, and it was headed right for them.

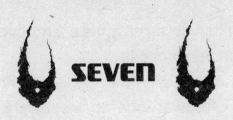 **SEVEN**

"Mata Nui preserve us," Dekar whispered, in shock.

He had seen a beam of energy shoot from the mask in the fraction of a second before his blow would have landed. It had lanced deep into the cave, disappearing into the darkness. Even as it did so, Kalmah got close enough to wrap his tentacle around the Po-Matoran. Dekar yelled in pain.

"You're out of your depth, Matoran," Kalmah said. "Destruction is our job, and —"

The Barraki's words were interrupted by a screech that grew into a roar that shook the ocean floor. Kalmah glanced away from the Matoran long enough to see a huge, dark shape hurtling toward him from the depths of the cave. Then something smashed into him, sending him tumbling uncontrollably through the water.

Mantax had hung back, so he was still outside the sea cave when it happened. He saw something moving — saw the Matoran and Kalmah demolished by a single blow — and then ducked aside. Something massive shot from inside the cave and up into the open water. Then it turned, its crimson and green eyes fixing on Mantax.

It was like nothing the Barraki had ever seen. It was a venom eel, but one easily 300 feet long, with jaws large enough to swallow the Matoran city whole. Slime dripped from its skin, raining down on the seafloor. It lashed out with its tail, striking the undersea mountain and sending a violent tremor through the caves beyond. Mantax barely got out of the way of an avalanche.

The Barraki had spent many, many long hours buried in sand, watching the sea life all around him. He knew everything that lived down here, or thought he did — how they thought, how they felt, what they needed to survive. But he could have been the barest novice, underwater for the first time, and he still would have known what the monster above wanted.

It was enraged. It was in pain.

And it was hungry.

Takadox emerged from his cave. He had felt the intense quake and was afraid it meant Ehlek had gone ahead and destroyed Mahri Nui. If his fellow Barraki had succeeded, the Mask of Life might be lost forever beneath the rubble.

When he saw the nightmarish creature, his keen mind realized what had happened. *Someone threatened the mask,* he thought. *And it protected itself. Its power reached out to an eel and made it grow . . . and grow . . . so it could serve as a guardian.*

Takadox staggered backward. Venom eels were evil and destructive by nature. Giving one more power was like giving a Takea shark sharper teeth. No good would come of it, and in this case, everything under the sea might be destroyed.

Unless . . . the Barraki said to himself, a tight smile creasing his misshapen features. *It's still just a dumb animal, and my powers are just made for use on dumb animals. Look at Carapar. If I could entrance it — get it to obey — then Pridak and the rest will be answering to me.*

Everything that lived beneath the ocean was fleeing from the creature the Mask of Life had created . . . everything but Takadox, who began to swim toward it, savoring thoughts of death and destruction.

Gar and Idris were out of air. They had moved as quickly as they could up toward Mahri Nui, but it hadn't been fast enough. They weren't going to make it to the city in time.

In desperation, Gar pointed toward the fields of air. It was their only hope. The two Matoran swam for the nearest patch of airweed. If they could salvage a bubble from the crop, it might hold them until they could make it back to the shelters.

They hit the field at the same time. One ripe stalk would be all they would need. There had to be one somewhere the hydruka had not harvested yet.

Then they noticed that something was very wrong with the beds of soil from which the air-weed sprang. The ground had begun to move. Gar backed away, gesturing for Idris to flee. What had looked like rich earth from a distance was anything but — the fields were infested with keras, all of them more than happy to see potential prey.

And the Matoran had one of those difficult choices life sometimes presents — was it better to drown, or be devoured?

Pridak was stunned at the sight of the monstrous venom eel. Defilak was as well, but he wasn't going to let that stop him from escaping. He swam off at top speed, heading for the edge of Mahri Rock. With luck, there would still be time to save Idris and Gar from imprisonment.

The Barraki took no notice of his captive's flight. He was no longer even paying attention to the monster bearing down on him. No, his attention was focused on the direction from which the creature had come.

This is no beast in nature, he thought. *Something made it this way. And that something can make me what I used to be. . . . Once it does, not all the power of the fates can save Makuta and Mata Nui from my vengeance.*

Pridak dove and swam, trying to evade the monster even as he followed the trail back to its lair.

Ehlek dragged Carapar down into the depths, hanging on to his claw. He ignored his fellow Barraki's protests. Of all the Barraki, Ehlek knew best just what a venom eel was capable of, and he did not want to see what a 300-foot-long one would do.

There were other reasons for flight as well. Pridak would no doubt be occupied dealing with the monster, since no shark could resist combat. That left his cave home unguarded. Ehlek had long believed that one of the Barraki betrayed them all to the Brotherhood of Makuta, all those years ago. If that was so, he had no doubt Pridak knew who it was and was just biding his time, waiting for the right moment to take revenge. Now was the time to find out for certain.

The two Barraki maneuvered their way through twisted coral reefs below the Pillars of Salt. Ehlek led the way into Pridak's cave, then stopped short — someone was already in there! He hurled an electric bolt into the darkness. It struck something and ricocheted, almost hitting Carapar.

The stranger charged. Carapar grabbed him with both claws while Ehlek maneuvered behind and tried to jolt the fight out of their opponent. He fought well, this mysterious new arrival, but he was obviously not used to combat in an underwater environment. The water slowed his blows, robbing them of much of their power. Eventually, the two Barraki pinned him against a stone wall. Carapar brought a claw close to the newcomer's throat, leaving no doubt what he would do with it given the chance.

"Who are you?" asked Ehlek. "What are you doing here?"

The stranger looked around, confused. Ehlek had seen that look before. Lifelong land dwellers had a hard time adjusting to life in the Pit. In most cases, the water mutated them rapidly so that they could breathe in the depths — if it didn't, the new arrivals rarely lived long. The Matoran of Mahri Nui were the exception, thanks to their fields of air. This one was hesitant to open his mouth, expecting to drown. Carapar dealt with that by slamming him into the rock a few times until he cried out.

Shock merged with realization on the stranger's features. There was water in his mouth, but he could breathe and he could speak. The knowledge seemed to restore his strength. He shrugged off the two Barraki and said, "My name is Brutaka. And you are some sort of sea monsters? How did you learn to talk, or are you just talented mimics?"

"We are Barraki," said Ehlek. "And you are in our territory."

"Ah, Barraki," Brutaka replied. "You were

important once, weren't you, a long time back? No matter — you'll answer to me now."

"As long as the question is 'Who's that killing me?'" Carapar shot back. "Then we should get along fine."

"I came from the island of Voya Nui," Brutaka continued, ignoring Carapar. "I was there to guard the Mask of Life, but I decided it would be better put to use in my service. My fellow guardian, Axonn, disagreed — and he had the stronger argument. When I woke up, I was underwater. I swam until I found a hole and eventually wound up here."

"The Mask of Life," said Ehlek. He went on to describe the mask that Carapar claimed was in the possession of the Matoran.

Brutaka's eyes brightened. "That's it. It's here! Amazing! Fate must want me to have it; there's no other explanation. And once I do . . . Axonn and I will resume our discussion. Take me to the mask — now!"

Carapar started to object, but Ehlek cut him

off. "Of course, of course. Only we have a little problem reaching it at the moment — actually, a 300-foot-long problem. But maybe you can help with that?"

"You may have a bigger problem than that," Brutaka answered. "If I am here . . . and the Mask of Life is here . . . then six Toa are not far behind."

The monstrous eel crashed into the peak upon which Pridak had been standing just a moment before, shattering it into rubble. Its mind and memories were a jumble. One moment, it was sleeping in its cave — the next, it was too big for its own lair. The cave had provided a safe haven from other predators, but now Tarakava and Takea sharks were snacks.

Its eyes were drawn to something glittering in the dark waters. Its dim brain couldn't know that what it saw were lightstones shining in the city of Mahri Nui, but it could smell prey. More, it caught the scent of other venom eels down there, thousands of them. No doubt they were after the source of the lights. Little did they realize that no one could deny the creature anything it wanted now.

Pridak, the Mask of Life, all were forgotten. The creature turned and sped toward the city, ready to feast.

# EIGHT

Gar wanted to yell for help, even though he knew it was a stupid idea. His air bubble was gone, and shouting would have just led to drowning. No one was near enough to hear and help anyway. Still, somehow it would have made him feel better if he could have let out a good yell at least once before he died.

He had fallen behind Idris. She was getting near the city, trying to avoid the venom eels that were swarming around the borders. Gar could feel the claws of the keras crabs snapping at his feet and legs.

A strong hand suddenly grabbed his upper arm. He felt himself being pulled along at high speed toward the city. Glancing up, Gar saw the familiar mask of Defilak. The Le-Matoran paused only long enough for Gar to grab Idris before resuming his rapid swim toward Mahri Nui. Venom eels who tried to get in their way were slashed aside by Defilak's blades. Only when the three were inside one of the large air bubbles that protected the shelters did Defilak slow down.

"Happy to look-see you are still breathing," he said.

"For now," Gar answered. "Or haven't you seen that monstrosity heading this way?"

"I've seen it," Defilak replied. "And you all wonder why we Le-Matoran *hate* the water?"

Takadox watched with a mix of horror and anticipation. The monstrous venom eel was dead on course for Mahri Nui, despite the hail of air spheres fired from the city and the hundreds of vampiric sea squid that had attached themselves to its massive body. The combination was not even slowing the creature down.

It slammed into one of the lower peaks, turned, and whipped its tail at the Pillars of Salt, shearing off the top of one. Then it headed for the city again, piercing one of the Matoran air bubbles and reducing a storehouse to rubble. It banked away and swam toward the surface, then turned to make another dive.

This time, it barely missed the Matoran buildings, but the impact sent a tremor through the entirety of Mahri Rock. The swarm of venom eels that had been besieging the city fled in panic. The keras crabs were not so swift or so fortunate. As it turned away, the creature opened its huge jaws and swallowed several hundred of the crabs as they tried to get away.

Magnificent, thought Takadox. *It would almost be worth losing the Mask of Life to gain control of such a beast.*

Even as the thought crossed his mind, the monster lifted its head and took notice of the Barraki. Takadox met his gaze, exerting the hypnotic powers the Pit had granted him. If all went well, in a matter of moments the beast would belong to him; body, mind, and spirit.

Dekar woke up. Every part of his body hurt. He wasn't sure what had happened or how much time had passed, or even why he was still alive.

Without moving from where he lay, he scanned his surroundings. He was still in the sea cave, the mouth of which was partially blocked by rubble. The only light came from the Kanohi mask he had brought with him with the intent of destroying it. It had also provided enough air to reinforce his bubble.

Dekar struggled to remember how he had ended up like this. He had been about to strike a blow to shatter the mask. Then there was some sort of flash of energy, and a monstrous creature, and —

It . . . it was defending itself, he realized. The mask knew what I was about to do, and it —

He pulled away from the Kanohi. It looked just like any other mask, but somehow the empty eye sockets seemed evil to Dekar. He could almost feel it watching him, waiting to lash out and destroy him if he should try to harm it again.

No. That's ridiculous. Get a hold of yourself, he thought. All right, maybe it's damaged . . . maybe somehow it can work even when no one's wearing it . . . maybe it even has some way to protect itself. But it's a thing — it can't be good or evil. It's just a thing, and it can be used — or broken — like any other thing. Can't it?

Dekar brought his hand close to the mask, moving as hesitantly as if he were reaching into the jaws of a shredder fish. *If I can just touch it — and if nothing happens — then I'll know I'm just being crazy. I'll know it's just a mask like any other, maybe a little more powerful, but . . .*

The tips of his fingers brushed the hard surface of the Kanohi. There was no second burst of energy, no new sea monsters, no sudden disaster. In some ways, to Dekar's point of view, what happened was worse.

The mask spoke to him.

No, it didn't talk like a Matoran did, or even form words in Dekar's mind. Instead, Dekar saw a jumble of images that swirled as if caught in the tide. With great effort, he made them coalesce into some kind of a comprehensible whole — it was do that or go mad.

Suddenly, he understood. He was seeing history through the mask's "eyes," and he had knowledge that no other Matoran had ever possessed.

The Kanohi Ignika, or Mask of Life, had come into existence not very long after the first Matoran ever walked through this universe. It was to be the first of the masks of legend, and in many ways, the most important — for the Ignika was the difference between life and death for everything that existed. Molded by the Great Beings who created the universe, heated in forges fiery beyond imagining, cooled in caverns of ice, it housed power that dwarfed that of any being — even those that had created it.

In its first days, it did nothing but sit inside the armored shell that had been crafted to protect it. Although it was the Mask of Life, it knew little of what that meant or even the reason for its existence. Then one day, one of the Great Beings grew curious about the mask. He opened the shell, reached in, and laid hands upon it.

The Kanohi reacted. It sensed this being was not the one destined to make use of it — still, it was willing to share its gift. The mask flooded the Great Being with life, so much that everything around him became alive. Furniture, equipment, the stones that made up the walls and floor, even the rays of light that illuminated the chamber became living, feeling entities. Each had needs and wants and each now found voice to demand them. It seemed to the mask a wonderful gift to bestow, especially on someone who prided himself on his ability to create.

Unfortunately, it had not proven to be a blessing. The Great Being reacted with shock and horror to his new abilities. Since the power was now part of him, he could not hope to outrun it. Eventually, the others of his kind had to step in and confine him so that he would stop bringing their inanimate objects to life. There were whispers of madness. After this, the other Great Beings treated the mask with less idle curiosity and more respect.

It was a short time later that two more of

the mask's creators came to transport it else-where. They were careful not to touch it, using special tools to handle its armored shell. They brought it to someplace far beneath the ground and placed it on a pedestal. A guardian, Umbra, was posted, and other traps were laid for the unwary. The mask, too, used its power to create additional guardians, transforming microscopic protodites into large, savage protodax, for example.

It waited. And waited. Centuries passed, then millennia, with only the occasional intruder making an effort to claim the mask. None ever made it past the guardians. Then a team of Toa arrived, led by a Toa of Magnetism. They battled their way past the guards and the traps and reached the mask chamber. The Ignika did not fight them — it could tell they were meant to use its power. They removed it from its pedestal and brought it to another place, where it was needed.

After the mission was done, the Toa were

left shaken and fearful of the Ignika. They returned it to its underground chamber and then transformed into smaller, less powerful forms. One, the former Toa leader, remained aboveground to watch over the mask, taking on the title "Turaga."

Many, many more years passed. The mask felt the universe rocked by some great cataclysm, though it knew not what. Over time, though, it began to sense disturbing disruptions in the patterns of life above. Something was wrong with the fundamental fabric of all existence. Beings had arrived on the surface who coveted the mask's power, while others journeyed toward its hiding place with noble intent.

Realizing the power of those who wished to seize it, the Ignika used its power to call one of their number to its chamber. The being, one called Vezon, attempted to take the mask and was cursed for his efforts. The Ignika fused itself to him, and then fused him in turn to a massive spider creature evolved by the mask's power. A new guardian had been created, although one more evil and less sane than perhaps the Ignika would have liked.

At the same time, the Mask of Life reached out with its power to the ones who came to use it for good purposes. It selected one of them — a Matoran named Matoro — as a potential future guardian. It tested him, and he proved himself worthy. When Matoro finally reached the mask, though, it was not as a Matoran but as a Toa. He removed the mask from Vezon, prepared in his heart to take it wherever it needed to go.

Here, at last, the Ignika rebelled. The time was not yet right to make the journey. The universe was still damaged, though not beyond repair. Not wishing to harm Matoro, the mask used one of its other guardians to free itself from the Toa's grasp. Then it flew to the surface and plunged beneath the waves, going to where it sensed the damage was greatest and hoping the Toa Inika would follow.

But something had gone very wrong. The waters were proving deadly to the mask. It had already begun to crack and crumble, energy leaking from it in the form of air. Hostile forces once more sought to possess it, and the Toa were facing great danger in their efforts to reach it. If they did not arrive in time, the Ignika might fall into evil hands, or worse, destroy itself completely in the toxic brew of the Pit.

For the first time in its 100,000-year existence, this awe-inspiring mask, this most unusual artifact of power, knew what it was to be afraid.

 **NINE**

Defilak, Gar, and Idris had gone mad — or so it seemed to the other denizens of Mahri Nui. With the fields of air cut off and the city menaced by a sea monster beyond all imagining, the three of them were swimming from place to place committing acts of vandalism.

"Smash them! Smash them all!" Defilak yelled. Then he swung his blade and shattered another lightstone, while the other two Matoran did the same. Working from one end of the city to the other, they broke every lightstone they ran across, plunging Mahri Nui into darkness.

"What are you doing?" Kyrehx demanded. "Have you lost your minds?"

"No, come to our senses," Gar replied.

"Venom eels — think!" Defilak snapped. "They react to light and movement. Douse all the light and this one won't see the city. Get everyone away from the borders and into shelters — especially the fortress. Anyone outside has to remain-stay perfectly still. The slightest motion will bring the creature back. Go!"

Kyrehx took off on her mission. She still wasn't sure she understood the plan — were the Matoran supposed to remain motionless and in darkness for the rest of eternity? And what about the invaders? With no one to guard the borders, what was to stop them from conquering Mahri Nui? But she supposed it made sense to face one danger at a time.

She herded the villagers into their shelters, while getting another group moving into the fortress. As she did so, her eyes were drawn to the peak in the distance. It was a most unusual geographic feature, even for this place, for the very top of the mountain extended toward the surface with a narrow cord of stone. The mountain was riddled with caves, but those few Matoran who had tried to explore them had never returned. She often wondered just where that cord led to, and if she would ever see the world above the waves. Now and then, she would get a flash of memory of living on dry land, but the flashes never lasted long. She dismissed them as fantasies.

"Come on, get moving," she said to a straggling Ta-Matoran. It was time to deal with reality again. Maybe later, if the city survived, there would be more time to dream.

The creature was troubled. Just moments before, there had been a lush, glittering hunting ground down below. Now all was darkness and stillness and it could no longer spot the site of its previous attacks. The only things moving were the keras crabs, and as small as they were in relation to its size, they barely constituted a meal.

Oh, there was one other thing in motion. It was a being that hovered in the water near the creature's face, staring into its eyes. The being had strange eyes. . . . There was something compelling about them . . . so that the creature did not want to look away . . . yes, best to keep staring so the being could not slip away without the creature noticing . . .

The venom eel suddenly started. It had heard a noise, then another and another, sounds that were not a natural part of the undersea world. They were coming from the stone cord atop the great mountain — no, they were coming from *inside* the cord. Was there some new enemy hiding in there? Or better yet, a meal?

This was much more interesting to the creature than the strange little being's eyes. It shot forward, heading toward the cord, and plowing into the being in the process. The monstrous eel swam on, paying no attention to the unconscious Takadox spiraling swiftly down into the black waters.

Pridak spotted Mantax first. The Barraki was swimming as if every creature of the Pit was chasing after him. Pridak intercepted him before he could dive into a sea cave.

"Our prey is the other way, is it not?" the

Barraki leader said. "Or have you forgotten, in the years we have been down here, how to advance *toward* a battle?"

Mantax hurriedly related all that he had experienced — the Matoran with the strange Kanohi, the monster that emerged from the cave, and his own valiant efforts to go find help for Kalmah.

"Help from whom?" Pridak asked, unconvinced. "The seaweed? The shells? That is all you will find here. Show me where this happened, and we will help Kalmah ourselves." Then he smiled, baring his wickedly sharp teeth. "Or at least make sure he does not go to waste."

The two Barraki made their way toward the cave where Dekar and the Mask of Life had been spotted. As they neared that point, Pridak's keen senses picked up the approach of others. Two of the scents were familiar — Ehlek and Carapar — and one was not.

Pridak signaled for Mantax to keep going while he circled behind. If there was a newcomer to the Pit, it might be someone else seeking the mask. In that case, Pridak would make short work of him. Someone else to share the loot with would not be a welcome sight.

He spotted them quickly. The two Barraki were swimming rapidly with the newcomer between them, barely keeping pace. He looked powerful. Pridak decided to take no chances — bite now, ask questions later, if the stranger was still alive to answer them. He moved in, silently, his jaws aching for the thrill of the first attack.

The stranger glanced over his shoulder. He spotted Pridak, but the Barraki was confident his prey had no time to react. Then a sizzling bolt of energy shot from the newcomer's sword and struck Pridak, sending spasms through his body. He managed to grab on to a rocky ledge and held on tightly despite the convulsions. If he sank to the bottom of the black water in this condition, he would never rise again.

When he regained control, he opened his dead eyes to see Ehlek, Carapar, and the stranger looking at him. *No doubt they were waiting to see if I would die, so they could get to me before the carrion fish did,* Pridak thought. *How disappointed they must be.*

"Who . . . is . . . this?" Pridak said, with some difficulty.

"He says his name is Brutaka," Carapar answered. "And that we work for him now."

"I have come for the Mask of Life," Brutaka said. "Anyone who tries to deny me my rightful due will be an obstacle that must be removed."

"I know . . . a little something . . . about removing," Pridak replied, letting go of the ledge and starting to swim again. "Arms. Legs. Think about it."

Mantax joined them. If Brutaka was concerned that the odds were now four against one, he didn't show it. He simply followed the Barraki as they made their way down to the sea caves.

Once I have the mask, it won't matter how many of them there are, he thought. *It might even be amusing to see what the power of the Ignika would make of these . . . monstrosities.*

* * *

The creature circled the stone cord, eyeing it with suspicion. The noises were still coming from inside. It sounded like many living things inside, not just one, and all of them locked in battle. The creature had no idea if the cord contained land animals, sea animals, Matoran, Toa, or something else, nor did it care. It did not believe in discrimination. If they lived, it would eat them, whatever they were.

But how to get at them? There were no openings in the cord large enough for a venom eel of its size. And it wasn't very likely the prey would be accommodating enough to come out where it could be eaten.

Then the bestial brain of the monster got an idea. It wrapped its coils around the portion of the cord closest to the top of the mountain and began to squeeze. It would take only the smallest exertion of its strength to shatter the cord and spill out its contents into the sea. Whoever or whatever was journeying through the cord was about to have their trip stopped dead.

* * *

The Barraki and Brutaka found Kalmah first. He was just recovering consciousness after the attack by the venom eel. Unlike Mantax, the experience hadn't left him wanting to find a safe haven. Instead, it made him that much more determined to get his claws on the mask.

"Spread out," Pridak ordered. "If the Matoran and the mask are still in that cave, there's no telling what other surprises might be waiting in there. Carapar, clear away some of that rubble."

The crab-clawed Barraki looked at Pridak for a long time before complying. Sometimes the group's "leader" forgot that all six of them had been rulers in their own realms. They were not servants to be ordered around. Of course, saying any of that wouldn't be wise if Pridak was anywhere within earshot.

Carapar pulled some of the rocks aside. He could see a mask glowing inside, illuminating the Po-Matoran who was holding it.

"Get back!" said Dekar. "I'll destroy it!"

Pridak glanced around. His army of Takea

sharks had begun to gather in the waters nearby. Then he turned back to Dekar, saying, "Is that mask really worth your life, Matoran?"

"You've probably seen what it can do by now," Dekar replied from the darkness of the cave. "Is it really worth yours?"

"Let me handle this," Brutaka whispered. Then he swam toward the cave, treading water where he knew Dekar could see him. "Matoran! You can see I am not one of these foul creatures — my name is Brutaka. I am a member of the Order of Mata Nui, an organization dedicated to following the dictates of the Great Spirit. If you give me the mask, I vow by Mata Nui that the Barraki will never get their hands on it."

Brutaka waited. Nothing he had said had been a lie. He was a member of the Order of Mata Nui, just a fallen one — and he had no intention of giving the mask to the Barraki.

Inside the cave, Dekar pondered. Was this Brutaka telling the truth? Was there any point in trying to resist, when the Barraki could just come in and take the mask if they wanted it? Should he just hand it over and hope they wouldn't kill him?

"No," he said finally. "If you were destined to have this mask, then you would have been the one to find it. You want it? Come and take it."

"Well handled," Pridak said to Brutaka, all the while signaling to Kalmah. "Order of Mata Nui indeed — who would believe that?"

"Stand back," Brutaka snarled. "I will go in there and get the mask myself."

"No," Pridak answered. "I don't think so."

"Right," Carapar added. "Save your strength. You're going to need it."

Before Brutaka could respond, he felt powerful tentacles wrap around his arms and legs. Despite his own great strength, he found himself being dragged away from the Barraki, helpless in the grip of a gigantic squid. He looked over his shoulder to see that the creature was pulling him toward the edge of Mahri Rock, beyond which was nothing but the black water.

"Wait!" Brutaka shouted. "You can't do

this! Do you know who I am? Do you know *what* I am?"

"Sure," Carapar replied. "Lunch."

The Barraki watched until Brutaka and the squid had disappeared. Then they turned their attention back to the cave. Carapar tore the rest of the rubble away from the mouth. Then Ehlek moved in, hurling electric bolts toward Dekar. One struck the Matoran, causing him to drop the Mask of Life. Pridak was there almost before it hit the ground.

"No," Dekar said weakly. "Please. You don't know what it can do. You'll destroy it . . . if it doesn't destroy you first."

"Oh, there will be destruction," Pridak answered. "Of that, I can assure you. But it will not be the Barraki or this mask that goes down to ruin — it will be the Brotherhood of Makuta, the Toa, and the Great Spirit himself!"

The Barraki reached out and touched the Mask of Life. It flared up, its glow filling the cave. Then the light grew brighter and brighter, spilling out of the cave and blinding the Barraki. Dekar shielded his eyes, but the intense light was still visible even through his hands. Incredibly, the light hit like a physical blow, forcing the Matoran against the wall. He could hear the Barraki yelling in shock and anger.

The light continued to grow. It spread across the entirety of Mahri Rock, throughout Mahri Nui, up the mountain peak and the stone cord menaced by the venom eel. It looked as if a sun had appeared beneath the waves to illuminate the entire ocean with a painfully bright white light.

Throughout the Pit, every eye was closed against the glow to keep vision from being lost permanently. Thus, there was no one to see just what the light did, or how it had changed the course of destiny.

THE OFFICIAL BIONICLE VIDEO GAME
FEATURING THE PIRAKA AND TOA INIKA

BIONICLE
HEROES

COLLECT LEGO PIECES TO UNLOCK
UPGRADES AND PLAYABLE CHARACTERS.

MASTER POWERFUL WEAPONS
AND SPECIAL ABILITIES

EXPLORE THE SECRETS OF
THE ISLAND OF VOYA NUI

IN STORES NOVEMBER 2006
WWW.BIONICLEHEROES.COM

TEEN
T
Fantasy Violence
CONTENT RATED BY
ESRB

PlayStation.2

PC
CD-ROM
SOFTWARE

NINTENDO
GAMECUBE

NINTENDO DS

GAME BOY ADVANCE